Originally published as *Een echte vriend* in Belgium and the Netherlands by Clavis Uitgeverij, 2020
English translation from the Dutch by Clavis Publishing Inc., New York

Visit us on the Web at www.clavis-publishing.com.

A Real Friend written by Jennifer Wolfthal and illustrated by Judi Abbot

ISBN 978-1-60537-582-3

This book was printed in June 2020 at Nikara, M. R. Štefánika 858/25, 963 01 Krupina, Slovakia.

First Edition
10 9 8 7 6 5 4 3 2 1

A Real Friend

Jennifer Wolfthal & Judi Abbot

Benny needed a new best friend.
His old best friend, Max, was
really starting to bug him.

It's true, they had fun playing
Alien Invaders together.
But Max took forever to play,
and Benny got bored waiting for his turn.

They liked playing hide-and-seek together.
But Max always wanted to hide,
and Benny hated seeking.

At lunchtime, Benny's mom would ask: "What will it be today, boys?"
"Grilled cheese with pickles!" Benny would say.
"Peanut butter and jelly!" Max would say.
Since Max was the guest, Benny got stuck with peanut butter and jelly, again . . .

At times, Max did laugh at Benny's jokes.
Other times, all he wanted to talk about was bugs.
Yuck! Benny hated bugs.

One day, while playing Alien Invaders, things took a turn for the worse. "It's my turn to play," Benny said, grabbing the controller.

"Wait, I'm not done yet," Max said, snatching it back.

"You always take forever," snapped Benny.
"Fine, I won't play then!" Max said.
"Fine, go home!" Benny said.
"Good! You're not my best friend anymore!" Max shouted.
"Good! I'll find a new best friend!" Benny yelled.

And that's just what he did.
That afternoon, Benny dug through the recycle bin.
He gathered a few odds and ends from under his bed.
He searched through his closet. And he emptied out his toy chest.

Then he got right to work.
He used a cardboard box here
and a stack of blocks there.
A broken yo-yo here and half
a slinky there. An empty bucket
here and a pair of gloves there.
He stacked, and glued, and cut,
and measured, and twisted,
and tied, and used up lots
and lots of tape.

At last, he added on the finishing touches—button eyes, an eraser nose, and a great big smiley face.

"I'll name you Jax," he said.

Life with Jax was positively perfect.
They played Alien Invaders together.
Benny never had to wait for his turn.

They played hide-and-seek together.
Benny got to hide every time.

They ate lunch together.
"What will it be today, boys?" mom asked.
"Grilled cheese with pickles!" Benny exclaimed.
Of course, Jax agreed.

And Jax laughed at all of Benny's jokes.
He never once talked about bugs.

After a while, things began to change.
Benny played Alien Invaders so long,
he started to look a bit alien-like.

He got tired of hiding in a closet while
Jax watched from the bed. *Maybe some
lunch will help cheer me up*, he thought.

But grilled cheese sandwiches were, well, getting a little boring.

And Jax even laughed when Benny wasn't joking. *This is getting a little creepy,* Benny thought.

One day, while playing Alien Invaders for the gazillionth time, Benny realized something.
He missed playing hide-and-seek the old way (even if he did have to be the seeker).

He missed peanut butter and jelly sandwiches, a little.
He even missed hearing about bugs, sometimes.
Most of all, Benny missed Max.
What if Max doesn't want to be my best friend again?
he worried. Benny stared at Jax. Jax stared back.
"I guess there's only one way to find out," he said.

Benny carefully loaded Jax into his little red wagon
and made the long walk to Max's house.
He took a deep breath and knocked.

When Max opened the door,
Benny gulped and said, "Max. I'd like you to meet Jax."
"Come on in," Max said, smiling. "There's someone I'd like you to meet too.
Lenny, say hello to my best friend, Benny."

Benny and Max spent the rest of the day playing together with their robots.
Just like real best friends do.